A QUEEN IS HOLDING
A MUMMIFIED CAT

A Queen Is Holding a Mummified Cat
is the eighth volume
in the *Essential Poets* Series
published by Guernica Editions.

By the same author:
The Dance, The Cage and The Horse, D Press, Montréal, 1976.

MARY MELFI

A QUEEN IS HOLDING A MUMMIFIED CAT

Guernica Editions

Acknowledgements

Poems in this book have previously appeared in the following publications: *Exile, Matrix, The Canadian Forum, Waves, end of the WORLD speshul anthology* (blewointmentpress), *Poetic Treasures: Past and Present* (Young Publications), *The Canadian Author & Bookman, Mamashee, The Montreal Writers Forum, Wee Giant, Boreal International, Poetry Toronto Newsletter, Writ, Harvest, Atropos, Hh, Origins, Versus* and *Toronto Life.*

Copyright © 1982 by Mary Melfi.
All rights reserved.

Guernica Editions gratefully acknowledge financial assistance from the Publications Section of the Canada Council.

Cover photograph by Pierre-Louis Mongeau.
Typeset design by Tanya Rosenberg at Type A, Toronto.

Guernica Editions
P.O. Box 633, Station N.D.G.
Montréal, Québec
H4A 3R1

Canadian Cataloguing in Publication Data
Melfi, Mary, 1951—
A queen is holding a mummified cat

(Essential poets ; 8)
Poems.
ISBN 0-919349-10-2 (bound). ISBN 0-919349-09-9 (pbk.)

I. Title.   II. Series.

PS8576.E43Q43   C811'.54   C81-090122-6
PR9199.3.M44Q43

Dépôt légal — 1ᵉʳ trimestre
Bibliothèque nationale du Québec
& National Library of Canada.

Table of Contents

WELCOME

ON MY RAFT

Preface

Mary Melfi's poems and prose-pieces seem to arise from the same isolation, solitude or loneliness which is the foundation of her psyche; a self-contained, closed world the rules of which are unique, similar to no one else's, rules which follow the logic of dreams and not that of public wakefulness. The name "surrealistic" is a misnomer to categorise the quality of her art which is way beyond it, she has to use that name only because, presently, there is no better expression to describe it. The words and sentences in her poems are also compromises between the inexpressible and the accepted usage of words and sentences, they are rather approximations inherent with optical (or psychological) illusions in which far-away things are seen to be near and vice versa, in which the past, present, future (and conditional!) tenses are interchangeable, in which facts and desires, sights and insights, the external and the internal reality are fused. It is the entangled, mysterious, twilight-world of the Jungle, impenetrable, yet swarming with life, organically connecting millions of rooted, crawling, walking, climbing, flying creatures into one breathing, self-renewing entity. Mary Melfi's solitude is not a quiet one; it is filled with voices and noises and vibrations and echoes.

Despite all the above, it is not only possible, but almost easy to "understand" her poems. Once one begins to read them, one becomes a stunned observer and feels the need to follow her into the twilight. This feeling is similar to that when one enters a dark room: first the eyes see nothing, then gradually get used to the darkness and soon one can see every single object clearly, what's more, move around, safely, in the room.

Mary Melfi is a unique phenomenon, in contemporary Canadian poetry, in general, and among the women-poets, in particular.

Robert Zend

THE LOBOTOMY

The Transvestite

Why the dead are God's underwear,
the mountains are his dresses
and the rivers are his shoes.
God cuts a good figure on earth.

Why with the rain washing his clothes,
with the snow dyeing them for Him
and with the earthquakes ready to give Him
a new change of underwear at a moment's notice

why human beings are just
the pupils of his eyes
or the eyes of the needles
his eunuchs use to embroider his clothes.

Why
when a mink comes my way
I will know that one of God's mitts
has finally dropped out of his hands.

The Lobotomy

Eternity or one of her mates
performed a lobotomy
on all the mountains and rivers.
The operations were unsuccessful.
They died. Eternity suffered remorse.
She laid all the mountains and rivers on her bed.
She has no more worries concerning their mental
    health.
(They will not lay their hands on her.)

Lobotomies were also performed
on all the animals, except mankind.
Take that slimy prince for example, the frog.
I do envy his sanity! Why with his love
for the sun and the mud that little bastard
is better off than all the kings of the world.
He is not waiting for a kiss from Ms. Eternity.
Eternity kissed the frog underneath her operating
    lights.

To gain favor with Eternity
I will feed the little tart half my brain.
I will pretend that neurosurgeon is sick
and my brain is medicine.

With half my brain missing
I'm bound to give up reading the obituaries
    (voraciously).

The Earrings of a Gypsy

Here's the symbol you've been waiting for: earrings!
Or is the symbol the old woman who is wearing the
  earrings?

The earrings are surely not the golden fleece or
  anything like it.
There's no legend behind them.

Ghosts have their own legends but an old woman
who is wearing golden earrings to attract attention
knows nothing about that.

The earrings rub against her shoulder blades
(unnecessarily exposed like the roots of an oak tree)
and that's obscene because she's too old
for that kind of love story.

Allow me to play hula-hoop with those earrings.
I'm the devil.

Those hooks which attach one part of her body to
  the other
are more expensive than the market allows her body
  to go for these days
(unlike the hooks in a butcher's shop which count
  for nothing).
I wish she were famous for her cooking but that's
  not the case.

She's just a symbol of mediocrity—
and that makes you mad as hell because you think
that's only my way of turning a legend into an inanity.

Let's Get to the Climax

Futility and I are multiplying.
        Her left nipple is a strawberry (comedy)
        and her entire right breast is made of cork
            (tragedy).
I adore her because she has taken away all obstacles
        (she is not an obstacle in my way by the way).
Futility and I meet (off stage) twice a week
        and my grandmother watches all this
        on her deathbed.

Look

That window isn't part of a mosaic
It's not covered with paper stars either
In fact there are no curtains

What's behind the window isn't amazing
It's not like an elephant or like a wild flower either

There's something behind it I'd prefer not to see
In fact I'd rather stare at a sink
than stare out that window

It's not useful
One look was enough to hurt my eyes
Another look might pluck out my eyes altogether

I'd better start thinking
of churches with stained-glass windows
I might need some help after all
to look out that crazy window

I can't avoid seeing its stains
I can't avoid being mortal

Of Animals and Men

Bones of animals are used
to make soups, jewelry, weapons and magic.

Our bones are never used.
Our bones only make for cemeteries.

I believe my bones are much finer
than the bones of any animal on earth.

So please never use my skull
in a recipe for DANGER.

The Loser

I lost more than a page out of my life
when failure chased me down a one-way street
and bit me.

I lost the ability to be sweetness itself.

I look at my face in the mirror
and read I used to be sweetness itself
but why I don't know.

The Chair

It wasn't the difference between
the colors of the sky and the palms of his hands
or the colors of the rainbow and the rain
or the colors of the eyes of his cat and his beloved's
which mattered in the end, the sick man decided.

He could remember the difference
between landscapes and horizons, between
    constellations,
between van Gogh and the rest of the Impressionists,
but he'd never be able to regain a sense of himself.

Ever since the doctor convinced him he'd go blind,
    for example,
he'd search out the blind in a crowd
but it wasn't the blind which held his attention
(he hated them the way he hated failure all his life)
but their canes.

He ought to have collected canes, he joked, not
    paintings,
maybe then he'd have succeeded in keeping at least
    one of his eyes
                   (for the masters).
                   Without them
he'd be reduced to a chair
(the cane would be one of its legs).

All his life the collector had believed
if someone (even miss fortune herself)
had tried to use him with such disrespect
he'd have been able to make the bitch fall flat on
    her face
and see all kinds of unpredictable colors.

A Welfare Recipient Talks to a Manikin

You and I are lovers
because you're worth less than a thought
and I'm worthless
because I'm armed with depression,
but no machine gun.

Talk to me, dear, I like you
because with no job, no man,
no guts to be merry and holy,
I'm only a beast and a burden.
Poverty is mending my clothes.

You're naked, but I'm so so hungry for the good life.
Half your body's missing but I've been jailed for
    shoplifting
so let's be comrades.

Help me, sweet nothing,
fill the ranks of the unemployed
with the same grace death slaps the face of a president.
Your smile smells like my ambition to be president.

Assassinate me, lady.
I'm ready to be shipped into your arms.

Or find me a job, miss shit house
and I'll ask the shopkeeper to throw you out on the
    streets.

The Invalid

My heart and my womb have been properly attached to my body. My ex-husband's heart, my mother's heart and an entire dead baby whose mother I knew as a schoolgirl have also been properly attached to my body. They're resting on the table beside my hospital bed in their proper glass bottles.

Liquids of all the colors of the rainbow (perhaps neon itself) are flowing into my bloodstream. My bed is surrounded by blue circles, gold circles, green and red circles of glass bottles. (I've been promised a blood transfusion as soon as the Red Cross workers call off their wildcat strike.)

A glass bottle huge as a man is resting in the corner of the room. I'm sure this bottle contains my husband as it is black and it makes ugly noises in the night. I guess the genie wants to cast off his vows.

A cord (with the colorings of a coral snake) attaches all the glass bottles to each other. Part of this cord is wrapped around my neck. In an attempt to pull the cord's head out of its electric socket I'd choke.

Doctors and nurses throng by my bed. "Here's a miracle!" they exclaim. "She's alive, the poor devil!" they exclaim. Humbug!

One day each one of them will throw a bowling ball down my body, down the bedside table and across the floor. They'll shoot down my multi-colored bottles and then play spin-the-bottle on my bed. I've seen more than compassion on the charlatans' jocular faces.

Three women, three insignificant victims, three specimens of infertility, of hope and of *rigor mortis* are also in the room with me. They're beautifully bandaged in foreign flags.

There's a mirror on the wall. It magnifies everything. There's a microscope hanging down from the ceiling like a house plant: a wandering Jew.

I can't adjust the wig on my head because all my fingers have been attached to wires. These wires are attached to a machine which rests with the head nurse in the other room. Each time she glances up from her Harlequin romance to check the data on the machine— dead or alive (a flashing olive light or a flashing violet light respectively)— she rings a bell.

I can't adjust the wings on my back (TV antennas) nor can I pull out the stinkhorns (*phallus impudicus*) growing out of my abdomen. I can't even smoke.

I won't be a lady.

Around Children's Territory
(Ha Ha's Pastime)

Around children's territory (Ha Ha's pastime)
some obese nuns are picking up forget-me-nots;
Nero, Hitler and the Devil are behind them (yawning).

I hover around companions who hover around the
   slogan:
By Hook or by Crook I Shall Be the Superior One.

> Dear priceless Factory,
>   Your eyes are on fire
> because you are beating me.
> Their eyes are on fire
> because they are beating me.
>   Your admirer,
>   1: 2,000,000,000

Hospitality

The next time you're at my house
I'll offer you two chairs, two handsome chairs.

You may seat your ridicule
(I hate to see it cuddled up in your arms)
in either of the two
but take care
as one of them will be an electric chair.

I Pour My Martinis into the Fishbowl

I'm not leaning against an iceberg
with binoculars around my neck, naked,
nor am I sitting on a sarcophagus, naked,
with a sword on my lap.

No, my eyes are just as good as binoculars
and my conversation is just as fine as an iceberg.

THE HEAD

I Watch His Love Climb Up My Body

I watch his love climb up my body.
"Is it possible to watch love climb onto its platform?"

There is no time to squabble.
It's here (like a cat muffled up inside a doctor's bag).

"Is his love giving your body back parts life took
    away?
Isn't it merely taking away all your body's
    belongings?"

There is no time to squabble. It's here.

Your Love Has Its Advantages

Your love has its advantages.
  It's better than a cane.
    It won't sit
      inside an hourglass
        and watch its components
          fall down yonder.
            No,
         it's much too busy
        holding up
      a lightheaded girl
    whose death warrant
  is being read by the eyes of the world.
The world is nailed to your bedposts.

30

Inside a Lobster Trap

Inside a lobster trap
        with a fishnet for a gown
            and angelfish for slippers;
the living room is a sea of hooks
        and this is my husband, the fisherman,
            who'd like to sell me off as a mermaid
                but who'd break his neck to enter me.

My Body's a Helicopter

My body's a helicopter
and I'm its driver.
As long as you know where you belong, darling,
and exactly to whom you belong, darling,
you're welcome
otherwise you better bring
a parachute rather than a goodnight kiss.

The Head

His head is sticking out of the river.
It looks like a life buoy. Someone threw it out of a
  boat.

Or maybe he placed the river over his head like a
  poncho.
It suits him.

His head is sticking out of the river.
Bedsheets also hide his body like that.

He looks greedy.
The river moves about him like a band of women in
  heat.

It's far enough to look like that:
his head looks like the head of a rhinoceros.

Just like a water-skier I hold a bar in my hands.
I'm on shore though. The line is attached to the
  rhinoceros.

It's made of wire. In fact there are two wires attached
  to its two horns.
Tiny little things are strung on one wire.

It's mostly fish but I swear there are a couple of dead
  babies
there too. I can smell those sly bastards.

There is nothing on the other wire. Maybe it passes
  through memories.
It's rusty enough.

That animal could pull me towards him.
I'll drown.

Please don't move farther away from me!
I'm alone with a picture of death.

His head is sticking out of the river.
The river around his neck looks like the collar of a
  guillotine. It sparkles.

That little head floating down the river dominates me.
The river needs a new head.

By the Swamp

You uproot a few reeds.
Decorations, you declare.
Just reeds, I answer.

You hit me with them.
I throw you into the swamp.

We argue.
Who has the more bruises?
We count them up
but it's no use.

We argue.
What's a decoration?
A bruise, a reed or a parting?

The Liar

Then he pointed out a fence,
an orange fence of no consequence.

Once inside its gates
we found a garbage can
in which an arm was sticking out,
his ex-wife's arm (he recognized
the bracelet and the ring)
waving an X-ray.

I grabbed the X-ray.
We hurried to his office to have a look at it.

"No mistake about it," I said,
add flesh to those two bodies
and you'll have lovers on that screen."
"Of course," said the doctor.

"Isn't that the lady who tried to unman you?"
"Myth," said my man.

The Spot

There's a spot on your face
(round as the lid on a garbage can).
The spot is less compassionate than a mating bird.
In fact, the spot is destroying the face I love.
I put on my sunglasses.
The spot is bloodthirsty
and just as pragmatic as the roof over my head.
It flies out of your face and breaks up our marriage
instead of breaking up the vacuum (cleaner?)
the world is using to brush its (sanguine) teeth.

A System of Lines: My Husband

His self-portrait consists of
horizontal and vertical lines.
I am there as a huge circle
he is carrying on his shoulders.

Each time I look at it
I discover something else about him.
"I escaped such simplification
a long time ago," he warns.

"Hold your tongue," I think,
"surprise is another form of violence."

When You Took Off

Rats took over my eyes
that is our house was overtaken by rats
when you took off
or rather my right hand took on the appearance of
   that pest
when you took off.

That very hand with which I used to close your eyes
and dictate *sotto voce* "I need no one" —
that hand had a rat in it.
I squeezed it to death because I missed you.

Jealousy

The problem is this:
I cannot avenge myself.

This time I see Susan
walking barefoot around our bed
through an instrument you have made for me.
I hate to have her here but
I cannot ask you to throw her out
because I have asked to understand you.
She is yours like your aging skin.
You don't need that instrument
to see your past, I do.

Susan sticks out her tongue at me.
She pulls a photograph out of her breast pocket.
You insult me.
Media, help me!

You fold up the instrument
because I simply cannot share you.

The Sword Dance

Swordfishes, swordsmen too, are equipped to get
    along in life
but I'm equipped to be a dancer on the stars.
Your love is my equipment.
I'm equipped for two hundred thousand sword dances
    on the stars.

I've no need for walking sticks.
I'm equipped to be a dancer on the stars.
Dump all the walking sticks into the sea.
Let the swordfish eat them for all I care.

I'm equipped to pick up stars—
your love is that versatile a thing.
In fact, your love makes all swordplay worthwhile.

Allow the world, that able but ill-tempered
    swordsman,
to cut off our heads. We'll be merry.
We're equipped with lots of tricks.
You and I, two starry-eyed lovers in one costume,
will face the world looking like a giant star.

An Old Musical

The sunset is dressed in pure red
and you are dressed in black and white.

You are about to take a bow on a staircase.
The sunset is about to take a bow with you.

You look like a prisoner,
a prisoner, a blackface, in an old movie
who suddenly finds himself climbing a staircase
with a chorus girl made up in feathers,
an embarrassed prisoner (un *évadé*)
who is clutching onto his garb for dear life.
It's all a matter of mistaken identity.
You know how to make me laugh.

It's all part of the ritual.
I'm wearing green velvet slippers
to enchance my supple nakedness,
yes, my agile nudity.
It gives color to our performance.

There's a bed
on top of the staircase
with a harlequin bedspread over it.

You call me by my maiden name.
You call me by my nickname (Papagena).
You make cooing sounds. Cooee!
I'll not christen our staircase— *The Tower of Babel*.

I'll catch you.
I'll tear off your gear, but you're a man.
I'll never succeed in undressing you to my satisfaction.

You bare your white teeth.
Without warning I take off my slippers.

You Are As Close to My Body As My Lust

You are as close to my body as my lust:

your feet are more wonderful than a bouquet of roses
your hands softer than a view of the mountain
your face holier than a school of fish
and your kisses mightier than a great book.

Thank God, you fit inside my body
like color fits inside my eyes.

I'm tired of being lost inside the imperial darkness,
stranded in the big arms of the bitch, mother nature,
    alone.

Allow me the comfort of knowing you are
more perfect than a visit to Mount Fuji
more delicious than my ambition to be honest in all
    things
and more delicate than my fingertips

because you are as close to my body as can be.

WELCOME

Welcome

My house is more important than my hair.
Here take my hair. Make a harp out of it.
My own delicious house remains over my bald head.

When all my friends have plotted to execute me
(as a snowman is executed) outside their houses
my own house will remember me.
My house, my country, will come and take me away.

Once outside their crazy borders
with or without a wig, my house, my hero,
will let my body pass through it like a comb.

Once in My Room

I become an antique,
a crib (one in each corner),
jazz, lightning,
a man in evening dress,
a traffic accident,
a memory,
a pair of scissors.

I draw a circle on my floor.
I pile my books on the circle.
I squat on my books. I sing.

The infants especially become me.

An Appetite for Life

It's a riddle.
I'm so neat otherwise.

I want a baby to come and clutter up my body.
It's beyond me.

I love my round face.
It's an everyday face.
It's familiar.
I can do what I like with my property.
I can bite my lips until they bleed.

I love the cracks in the walls of my house
because I know them for what they are.
I've grown old with them.

I hate new cities.

I want a newborn to come and clutter up my life.
  Why?

The baby is the new clock I want for my bedroom.
Here is the alarm clock, darling. Dust it.
Is that the conundrum's first wrong answer?

The baby is a new untameable animal, the new me.
Let it come and pounce on the world.
I'm tired of living with a pile of textbooks in my arms.
I'm tired of explanations.
I'm a good woman.

I have a secret though.
My life does not lie on top of me at night like a
    blanket
or rest beside me. There's just a man with a round
    face there.

At night I hang up my life on top of the stars.
I'm afraid someone will creep into my room in
    the middle of the night,
turn my life into a thousand moth balls
and then shoot the moth balls onto a golf course.
I'm suspicious by nature. I'm rude too. I'm fussy
    about everything.

I'm worse off than a rape victim.
I will allow a tiny stranger to turn my own flesh and
    blood inside out.
Why do I dare? Why do I insist
on showing the world the insides of my body?
    Why mummy?
I'm better off than a necrophiliac, I hope. I'm sure.

It's not a myth either.
Once the loafer will swell up my body I will love it
because its mess, the half round mess, will be familiar
   to me.

I'll justify even the chaos inside my body, that superb
   enigma.
I'm precise. I've taken out a life insurance policy.
I'm impatient with miracles.

I can't guarantee my baby will be able to hang up its
   life
on top of the stars beside mine at night.
The nights are lighthearted but ephemeral;
the stars plain lightheaded.
I can't even guarantee my baby wholesome feet and
   hands.
I'm helpless.

I want a baby to come and visit my body.
It's all a mystery to me.

Pregnancy

My womb used to be as simple as a glass jar
but an upside down jungle and an arrow got in it.

It had better behave as this mother's property
and forget about being a wild jungle with an arrow in it

after all is said and done.

Your Body

Your body used to be as fine as seaweed
but now you have a cargo, Cynthia,
and so you are boat-like.

Here in My Arms

It's better than holding a telephone
or a microphone in my hand,
much better than holding a pair of sunglasses
(or catching sunlight)
or holding a grocery bag in my arms.
It's even better than clutching
a purse stuffed with diamonds and pearls
because that's comfort
and comfort isn't more alive than I am— like sawdust.
This is alive. This is my baby and I need her to be
    here in my arms.

Peace and Joy Free of Charge

My mother is superior to all the cathedrals
I saw on my last European trip.

In comparison to my mother
the cathedral's Renaissance Madonnas are as sacred as
a parade of Hollywood movie stars at the Academy
    Awards,

and as for their early Christian mosaics
my memory is able to compose better ones
of my mother sitting at the kitchen table.

Heaven is nowhere to be seen inside those cathedrals.
Heaven is akin to a durable womb.

My mother can scold me, embrace me or embarrass me
                    (in her own rococo style)
but I know it is her old job to make
                    peace and joy ready for me
                    at a moment's notice.

There's a Rainbow around Your Neck

It comes as a revelation.

All other women on this street,
this undoubtedly Canadian street,
are wearing winter scarves around their necks
but here you are with a rainbow around yours.
A piece of its cryptic tail is sliding
off your neck and onto the sidewalk.

You asked the rainbow to come and sit
around your neck, your aureate neck, for my sake?

For my sake, Aurora, agree with me:
                              the apocalyptic rainbow
(and I didn't place it around your neck
in honor of your apotheosized status)
bears witness to the fact that
you're my one celestial friend on earth.
                              An anomaly! An anomy!

However, my dear maverick, a rainbow
will not wear well around a neck, a *frostbitten* neck.

At Three O'clock Springtime

At three o'clock springtime
three to four to five year olds
(except one) were throwing happiness
at their apple-faced guardian.

Miss Apple Worm was throwing
frowns and a number of skulls
into a puddle of water.

Except one was picking up the skulls
for Miss Apple Worm.

The Carousal

You're a trespasser.
You're a fugitive.
The carousel is your best hideaway.

You mount the horse on the carousel.
Its saddle is decorated with rubies.
You're a noblewoman.
The horse is in your command.
You're galloping all over the world.

They're there.
They're there by the gate.
They've followed you.

You hear
the word,
mamma,
go off
like a siren.

You whip the horse.
The horse gallops faster.
You whip the horse.

They're there.
Your husband is at the head of the line.
"She's on the carousel," he shouts.

They've found you.
They've found you
galloping all over the world like a fool.

They look like twelve knights.
Twelve knights prepared for a tournament.
Who'll win your horse? Your property? Your kiss?
One of your relatives? One of your friends?
   Your employer?

They're walking towards you.
They're holding hands.
They're handcuffed!

You hear
the word,
mamma,
go off
like a siren.

You whip the horse.
It bleeds.
Your horse is a magic horse.
You press all its rubies.

Your carousel turns
like a spinning top.
Like a spinning wheel.
Like a wand.

They're there.
They're around your carousel in their proper positions.
One o'clock. Two o'clock. Three o'clock.
All the twelve hours are there.

The word,
mamma,
goes off
like a siren.
It's midnight.

Listen.
They're calling your name.
Look. They're blowing kisses.
Look. They're extending their arms toward you.

Look. They're addressing the wooden figures aboard
    your carousel.
Your baby addresses the wooden grin,
your husband the magician crouched on all fours on
    your left.

Admit it.
No one knows where you are.
No one knows who you are.
You're alone.

They want to jump
aboard your world.
Yours!
You're furious.

You whip the horse. It bleeds.
You press all its buttons in vain.
You cut off its old head with your sword.
You twirl its head on the end of your sword.
You're a court jester and
your carousel is a flying machine.
"Spin faster," you command.
It spins. It twirls. It twists itself. It spins faster.
It flies like a bird. A magic decoy. A predator.
Your horse is galloping around the moon. Vertigo!

You're a witch.
You're dizzy.
You've got a headache.

Where are the rubies?
Where's the magic?
Will-o-the-wisp?
Your carousel falls flat into the sea.

They're there.
They're there by the shore.
They're holding life buoys.

You hear,
mamma.

The wooden figures
aboard your carousel turn to life.
They're alive!
The beasts of burden salute you,
even the skeleton on board salutes you.
They address you by your first name.
You feel like a fairy queen.

You swim towards the shore.
You have the courage to swim towards your rescuers.

First, the judge aboard your carousel drowns,
then the waitress drowns by your side.
By the time you reach the shore
all your twelve companions are dead.

Look. They're not holding life buoys.
Look. They're holding miniature carousels in their
    hands.
They're holding the twelve keys to your heart.

They turn and twist,
turn and twist the twelve keys,
the twelve carousels inside you.
It's time to go to work.
To be loved you have to follow their commandments
(addressed to those who drowned at sea) to the letter.

The word,
mamma,
goes off
like a siren.
You're tired.

You wish
all the hours
of your life
were birds.
Were scavengers
and facetious.

Father
looks
like
a fog
and
mother
looks
much
like
a foghorn.

ON MY RAFT

On My Raft

On my raft

I used the arms of a manikin
to push myself onwards.

But then my destination
took on the shape of a cat.

It sits in the bathtub and
occasionally bleeds for Miss So and so.

At the End of the Road

Are those runners
I am running towards but

the trees on both sides of the road
are falling,

> a row of hunchbacks
> in the middle of the road
> are bowing because
> I am running out of breath

> and a row of women on one side of the road
> are desperately leaning towards
> a row of men on the other side
> like in a fairy tale out of print.

I am running underneath a bridge
made out of artificial limbs or hope.

So someone somewhere honks in warning.

An Exile

Here are the masks
or are they the faces?
The faeces of my own God? The God of the West?
Here, there and around my car, my nimbus, my prize,
here are the mountains named Fear.

I honk the horn of my car, a cougar,
   my sweet American cougar.
I honk. Will my honking (a sure lamentation)
inspire the God of the West (a mountaineer?) with pity?
I'm afraid, thoroughly afraid of these mountains
because their mouths are wide-open
and I can easily slip into their void
because the God of the West is crying.
(Or is it vomit?) It is dark.

Sacrifice my car?
Let the mountain God of the West chew it to bits?
Or should I kneel with my hands over my heart
and wait (with a license to wait, an exile)
for my fear to pass out of my body and into the night.
Let the night of the West fall over the cliffs.
Let the sun of the West (a ghoul?) clean up its mess
   in the morning.

I'm an Easterner. God of the East, help me.
Which is the way home? I want my city back.
I want my hustle and bustle. I want my city lights.
I want my Montréal. Mother, I'm afraid of the God of
    the West.

Are those stars (Where are their light switches?)
the misplaced eyes of this mountain God?
Eyes which came out of his bowels
and which the sky picked up
because even God's bowels
are worthy of a show in the West.

A light show! Off-Broadway! Unpeopled!

Your avaricious eyes, God of the West,
have the gall to be more beautiful than my old city
    lights back East
when all I want of them, of you,
are the right directions?

   Where can I find a hotel, Mister?

Look they're blinking. They're making eyes at me.
What are they saying? I'm only a city dweller.
"Cross on the green light," my mother told me.
What do you say, God of the West?
Where is my home?
Stop.
I can't hear your answer.
Am I lost?
Follow the yellow brick road?
It swings to the right?
It's dark.
Red, green, yellow rules useless, *ma mère*.
Flags ludicrous. All laws useless.
I'm alone, an exile, an expatriot, a citizen of fear.
God of the West, take pity.
I'm only a city dweller with an I.Q.
(of 2001?) — a globule, a drop of vomit, on your face.
Please don't wash me off the face of the earth.

Driving alone on a mountain dirt road in the West
at 35 miles per hour: fact No. 1.
It's raining: fact No. 2.
But fog lights on: fact No. 3.
Gasoline tank half full: fact No. 4.
Seat belt fastened: fact No. 5.
Watch out for the spooks, kid.
You're in the middle of nowhere.
Swish. Swash. Horn working: fact No. 6.

Stop.
Remember the God of the East.
Its colors?
Green? Yellow? Yes.
Oxblood? Yes. French? Yes. Stop.
Exit. Exile. *Ma mère est morte.*

GO WEST.
FIND YOUR OWN GOD.
MAKE YOUR EXIT, CANNIBAL.
WE DON'T WANT YOU HERE. GO.
MAD DOGS AND ENGLISHMEN, GO.

Exile. I? Or are you a cannibal, an intrepid
master of ceremonies too, God of the West?
Am I a piece of meat and metal
(without even a star on my forehead) on your altar,
your table, your mountain? Yours. Take me.

Without the sanctimonious kiss of the God of the East,
without even a mask of my ex-country to embrace
with only a puerile fondness for mother death
 and the wheel of my car
I'm ready to fall over a mountain cliff.
 A nocturnal exercise!
Hi, bridegroom! Take me quick, my aboriginal lover.
Make me shine. Turn me into a star tonight.
 A star of the West.

No! No, I'm not ready and that was the whole point
in asking: where's a hotel, Mister? Further West?
Stop.

I envy the mountain climbers.
A mountain is a mountain is a woman perhaps
 to impregnate.
To force birth out of — a kingdom of dignity and
 stardom!
There's no God of the West. No God of the East.
No black magic, no wars, no words to speak of
 when climbing. The world.

So bring me a mountain climber. Quick.
English or French. Black and White. Who cares?
Let him force life out of my fear.
I'm hungry. I'm cold. Rock me. Oh God

I wish my mother's womb (Stop)

were a pair of gloves (Stop)

I could buy back at a pawnshop (Stop).

I wish the God of the East (Stop, thief),

Québec, *mon pays,* were here with me.

Here, there and around my car,
here, there and around these mountains
   like thousands of Christmas lights.
With French shops, with English shops, with neon
   signs:

> GODS AND COUNTRIES ON SALE
> ON FIFTH FLOOR.
> JAPANESE MAKE. AMERICAN MAKE.
> RUSSIAN MAKE.
> WATCH YOUR STEPS, LADIES AND
> GENTLEMEN.
> CANADIAN MAKE OUT OF STOCK.
> THE SHOW MUST GO ON, CHEZ NOUS.

I would feel right at home.
I wish upon a star I were home.

The Reception

Only self-pity receives me at the airport.

I throw paper airplanes ahead of me.
I'm a prime minister and they're my bodyguards.

Mirror Mirror on the Wall

If a horde of flamingos
were to walk out of my mirror
while I was combing my hair
I'd stop everything.
I'd be content to watch their show

but what's there in the mirror,
that spy, is just another container
which I throw about from room to room.
I aim it perfectly in front of the television set
with or without its wrappers.

I hate to see that container,
that colossal can,
combing its hair,
copper wire,
but I'd never hate to see flamingos.
Whose fault is that?

I'd love to remove
television's made-to-order goddesses
out of their containers
in order to give myself
a set of bodies
with which I could meet the mirror,
that Garden of Eden.

If a horde of men
were to break through my mirror
holding television cameras in their hands
ready to knock me down
or electrocute me
I'd attempt
to protect at all costs
what I behold in the mirror
(rustproof like a fairyland's staircase).
Because it's not empty it's fragile.

Though Dreaming Is My Business

I'll sit on no moon,
   ladies and gentlemen,
      and wave my handkerchief
      in distress.
   I'll sit on no plastic moon,
   translucent or transparent,
on no cardboard moon
opaque or minute,
   or moon made out of dough.
   I'll sit on no moon,
      ladies and gentlemen,
         suspended from a ceiling
      in some psychiatric ward
   and have the likes of you
gape at me.
You'd like to see me,
   ladies and gentlemen,
      sit naked on a moon
         or on a huge lightbulb,
            an iridescent lightbulb,
      in The Queen Elisabeth Hospital's
psychiatric ward.

You'd like to see me
in that unlucky moonscape
with moonflowers,
  moonfishes,
    moonseeds,
      moonwarts,
    moonstones
  and dead luna moths
on my lap.
You'd like to see me
  pushed as if
    I were on a swing,
      a baby's swing.
        You'd like to see
        the queen's lunatics
      push me
right out of the window
and into the moonlight.
  Don't deny it,
    ladies and gentlemen.
      You'd like to see
        this moonfaced lady
        look up at the moon
      and cry,
"Hail Luna!"

You'd like to see me
  take my first lunar step
    towards that goddess.
      You'd like to see
        nighthawks,
        night herons,
      nightingales
    and loons
fly at me.
  I'll sit on no moon.
    I'm not moonstruck,
      ladies and gentlemen.
        I'm not hit with moon blindness.
      I've no need for braille or Moon type.
    I can read and write like all of you.
  You'd like to catch me breaking the law.
You'd like to catch me making moonshine
  or moonlighting,
    but there is nothing moony about me,
      ladies and gentlemen.
        You'll never catch me playing
        hopscotch in a cemetery
      under a full moon.
    You'll never catch me tossing
a lunate bone on any grave.

I'm lucid.
   Give up.
      Take your families
         on a trip to the moon.
      Go first class.
   Use up all the lunar modules.
Take some belladonna with you
in case boredom hits you hard.
   Or blow up the moon,
      dear loonies.
         What do I care?
           I don't need it.
      I can read,
   write
and dream
better than you all.

In the Crowd's Image

The room is full of snakes. The poisonous ones are in glass boxes; the others are crawling all over the room. They're part of the show. I'm in the show. I'm the star. It's a horror show.

Blonde hair, a doll's hair, is hanging down from the ceiling. The room was constructed inside a doll's chest. The doll's face is facing the sky. What a setting! It won an award for the architect.

Eyes, sheep's eyes, are also hanging down from the ceiling— mobiles. Their eyes open and close. I don't know how that is done.

The walls of the room are painted green. It's a pastoral setting— until the snakes are shot. I shoot the snakes. It's part of the show. One death for each customer.

There are no windows. There's just one door, a door a quarter of my size in one of the walls in the room. Nuns are posted at the door. They're also part of the show.

There are mirrors in the room. In some of them I'm a dwarf, in some I'm a giant, in some I've got two pairs of heads. I see every kind of being in those mirrors except what I remember myself to be like. When was the last time I saw reality face to face? I'm too old to remember.

I'm lying down on a table in the center of the room. The instruments of torture are laid out on the snakes' glass boxes. Nine chairs have been placed around the table. It's only fair. Nine is a fair number. Let the nine in. Pipe in laughter. Bring in my supper. I'm hungry. Let the show begin.

No one is here yet. Even Delia, our ticket lady, hasn't arrived. She'll sit down in her ticket box like a buddha. It adds to the atmosphere her sitting down like that. The nuns are at the door, but they're always there. They're deaf-mutes.

My head is shaved. On my skull are written in red the words *cerebellum, pineal body, cerebral cortex, thalamus, pituitary* and *pons medulla*. There are arrows pointing to the exact place where all those things can be found underneath my skull. We can't expect the members of the crowd, be they members of parliament, members of the Chamber of Commerce, members of the Ku Klux Klan, to be neurosurgeons at a moment's notice. We priced our tickets at $2.50. That's cheap. We're bound to get a mass of underprivileged children to boot.

What rumpus! What pandemonium! They're here. It's a big crowd. Delia is in her box. Poor devil! I used to sell tickets, now I'm the star.

They're waiting. They're anxious to get their money's worth. Just like in Nero's times. Remember the martyrs?— but I'm a star, I'm paid well.

It's a modern crowd. It's sophisticated. They're dressed up for the occasion. Some are in white tuxedos, some in black. Some of the women are wearing their country's native costumes. It's a modern crowd. They want to participate in the horror. We'll let them participate. Let the crowd come in, Delia. Let the show begin.

It's more than a show. It's better than Rembrandt's show of corpses. Better than a horror movie. It's an experiment. It's a show for the scientists. It's a show for a modern crowd.

Let's begin the ceremony. Let that crowd that files past me on the street like a train, like a cargo boat, like a jet plane, like a time bomb let that same crowd come into my domain. I'm the star. One death for each one of my customers.

Pipe in the laughter, Delia. Let the first nine customers crawl into my room (it's my room after all) and let the rest wait outside my door. Let them anticipate the horror and the blood. Let them!

Let my first nine customers enter my kingdom. Let them sit around me. Let each one of them examine me.

Be they Jewish, Catholic, Protestant, Hindu, pantheist or atheist (the atheists will come in naked to show their contempt for organized religion), let them each have a turn to play God. My body is clay. My spirit is clay.

Let them turn me against myself. Let them turn me into what they think I should be. In the spit image of their fathers? Their mothers? Their idols? Give them a chance to turn me into an image of themselves. Give them a chance to play God.

I'm ready. Don't be shy. Recreate me. Reconstruct me. Change me. Hurry. Use all the instruments at your disposal. Use all the horror you need. I'm insured. I'm a star. You've got two minutes and a half. Hurry. The others are waiting.

I'm ready. I'm ready to disintegrate. I'm ready to please all of my nine friends. Hurry. I'm ready to give myself up. Yes, squeeze me and I'll cry. Open my legs and I'll laugh, yes. Yes, open and close my eyes.

The Birdhouse

I will burn down my house
before I will allow the world to be hammered into it.

Rather delight in the old holes in my body
than have the world create a new one, a grave one, one
by which I will recall the whole of my life to have been
        a ludicrous chase
        (with a saffron apron around my waist
        and a songbird on my head)
        a lugubrious chase
after that very world which was designed to be no
  better than a nail
        from the very start.

        In the final chase
        the chaste holes in my body
        will be chased right out of my body
        and into the underworld. Amen.

Then use the world to nail my skull to a tree.
Paint it red, white and green.

Now I will use the blessed holes in my eyes to study
  my property.

ALSO AVAILABLE FROM GUERNICA EDITIONS

ESSENTIAL POETS SERIES

Marco Fraticelli	INSTANTS
Antonio D'Alfonso	QUEROR
	BLACK TONGUE
Jane Dick	CONCEPTIONS
Filippo Salvatore	SUNS OF DARKNESS
Axel Soestmeyer	RUSH OF WINGS
Daniel Sloate	A TASTE OF EARTH,
	A TASTE OF FLAME

COLLECTION SOURIRE

Richard Bouchoux	ANIMOTS

Please write to
Guernica Editions, P.O. Box 633, Station N.D.G.,
Montréal, Québec H4A 3R1 for our brochure.

Imprimé aux Presses Élite Inc.